CARMEN
SANDIEGO™

Based on the Netflix original series
teleplay by Greg Ernstrom

Etch is an imprint of Houghton Mifflin Harcourt Publishing Company.

hmhbooks.com

Designed by Jenny Goldstick and Stephanie Hays
The type was set in Proxima Nova.
The sound effect type was created by Jenny Goldstick.

ISBN: 978-0-358-38019-1   paper over board
ISBN: 978-0-358-38018-4   paperback

Manufactured in China
SCP 10 9 8 7 6 5 4 3 2 1
4500799966

CARMEN SANDIEGO™

THE CHASING PAPER CAPER

A GRAPHIC NOVEL

HOUGHTON MIFFLIN HARCOURT

BOSTON   NEW YORK

WHO IN THE WORLD IS
CARMEN SANDIEGO?

FORMERLY KNOWN AS:

Black Sheep

OCCUPATION:

International super thief, super sneak, expert fighter, gadget guru, mistress of disguise

ORIGIN:

Buenos Aires, Argentina

LAST SEEN:

Sydney, Australia

I was found as a baby in Argentina and brought to Vile Island, where I was raised as an orphan but I longed to set out and see the world.

I couldn't wait to train at VILE's school for thieves. I wanted to become a VILE operative, traveling the world to steal precious goods.

But I knew I had to escape after discovering what VILE really stands for: Villains' International League of Evil!

My new mission: securing the world's historic treasures from VILE.

Player

White-hat hacker

BACKGROUND:

Player is a teenager from Niagara Falls, Canada. He met Carmen by hacking into her phone while she was still at VILE.

SKILLS:

- Learns everything about every place that Carmen goes to help guide her on capers
- Remotely deactivates security systems
- Scours the web for secret signs, coded messages, and hidden clues about VILE's next moves

ACME

Agency to Classify and Monitor Evildoers

The members of this top-secret law enforcement agency are the only ones who know that VILE even exists. They suspect that Carmen has some link to VILE and are always hot on her trail.

Chief ACME's formidable leader has been pursuing VILE for years and thinks that Carmen may be the key to finally catching them. Often appears as a hologram.

Chase Devineaux

Formerly an agent of Interpol, Chase was recruited by ACME to finally catch Carmen, but is always one step behind her.

Julia Argent

Brilliant detective Julia Argent is the first to suspect that Carmen may be working for good.

Where next?

Poitiers, France
Red-handed

Amsterdam, Netherlands
Caught in the act!

We may have both been right about Carmen Sandiego.

Villains don't always look like villains, nor heroes like heroes...

Location: Mumbai, India • Time: 0900 hours

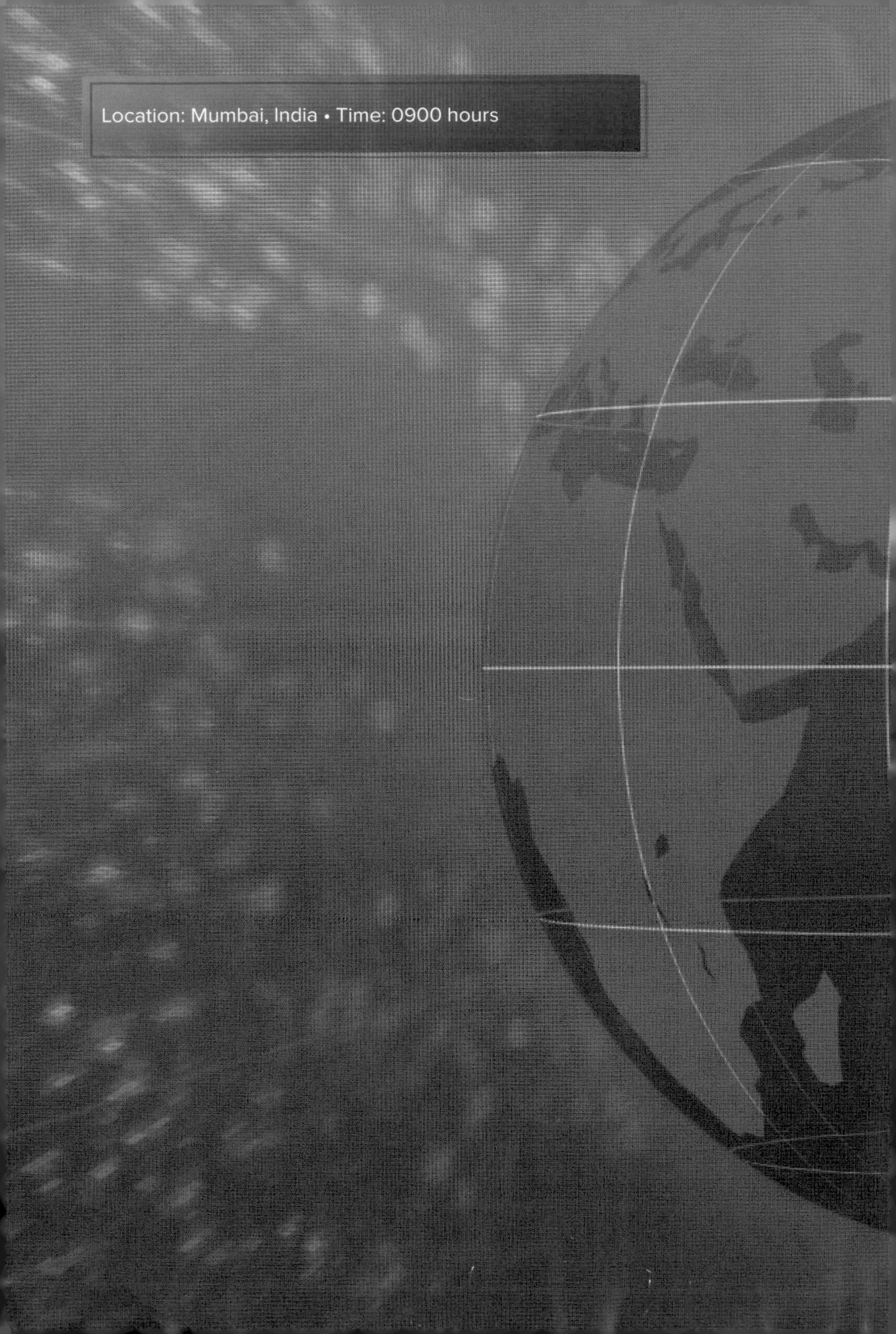

You sure about this, Red?

I'm not picking up chatter about VILE operatives in India from any of our usual sources.

At an outdoor café, Mumbai, India

Carmen views the museum over the rim of a teacup.

They'll be here. I know how Professor Maelstrom's twisted mind works, and he'd never pass up an opportunity like this.

Stealing the Magna Carta would be VILE's way of symbolizing that evil can triumph over law and order -- at least, that's what they'd tell themselves.

I think I see what you mean...

1215 CE

In the year 1215, England was ruled by some guy named John -- and if he were alive today, he'd probably feel right at home on Vile Island with your former teachers.

King John figured he could take anything he wanted just because he was in charge, and he abused that power constantly.

The archbishop of Canterbury stepped in and helped shape a set of laws that gave citizens rights --

-- basic stuff, like you can't be arrested for no reason, or have your horse taken away from you just because the king wants it.

These combined laws were named the Magna Carta -- Latin for "the Great Charter of the Liberties." It was the chief cause of democracy in England...

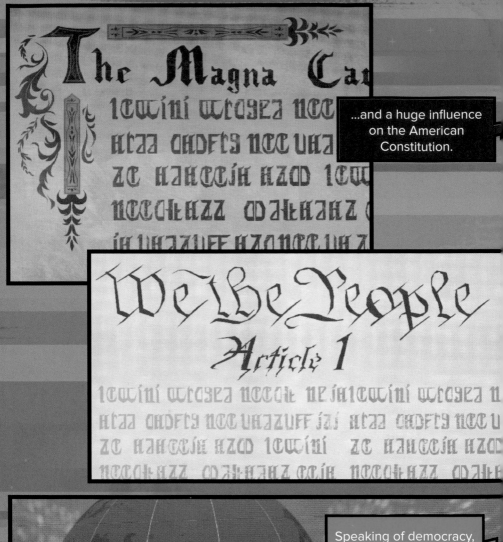

...and a huge influence on the American Constitution.

Speaking of democracy, India has more people than any other democracy in the world.

Which is where you happen to be sitting right now.

And since I favor democracy over tyranny, VILE won't be sinking their mangy claws into any historic documents on my watch.

I'll do one last perimeter check tonight, see if I can find any weak links VILE might exploit.

VILE Academy, Vile Island

VILE
Academy Instructors

Gunnar Maelstrom

A psychological genius, Maelstrom learns your weaknesses and twists your mind.

Countess Cleo

Cleo believes that ultimate wealth is ultimate power. She adores expensive everything.

Shadowsan

A real-life modern ninja, Shadowsan teaches the criminal power of stealth and discipline.

Dr. Saira Bellum

Death rays, invisibility fabric, brain-wiping machines -- these are Bellum's favorite things.

Coach Brunt

Master of hand-to-hand combat, Brunt believes a butt-whooping is the solution to everything.

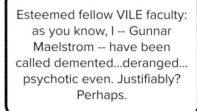

Esteemed fellow VILE faculty: as you know, I -- Gunnar Maelstrom -- have been called demented...deranged... psychotic even. Justifiably? Perhaps.

Inkblots slowly morph into different shapes behind Maelstrom as he continues to speak.

But I feel these are merely labels --

-- "safe" ways to categorize my unique intellect, which enables me to see opportunity where others do not.

So allow me to draw your attention to THIS, the very foundation of law and order in the Western world.

Looks more like a lion cub sniffin' its own tail if you ask me.

Wrong slide.

This -- the Magna Carta!

The Magna Carta

You're sayin' words I don't understand.

Coach Brunt, I suspect you are familiar with the US Constitution?

Darn right.
I'm Texas proud.
Think of the Magna Carta as the British version of it -- written more than 500 years earlier.
The Magna Carta
And for the first time in history, every known original copy of the historic document -- all 17 of them -- will be on display under one roof, here...

...at this renowned museum in Mumbai, India.

Which means we have an opportunity to steal them -- in the name of law and disorder.

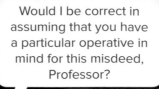

Would I be correct in assuming that you have a particular operative in mind for this misdeed, Professor?

The crime involves stealing paper, does it not?

She is far from ready.

Questioning my sanity after my compelling intro, dear Shadowsan?

Carmen Sandiego was unruly and undisciplined when she was a student here...and your newest star pupil is cut from the same cloth.

Shall we vote? All in favor...

At the museum, later that night...

Carmen crosses the museum roof with focused determination.

Ready to shut down the security cams, Red?

Carmen is transported to her past at VILE Academy.

She was at VILE Academy during my "hold over" year.

Paperstar

- Real name: Unknown

- Master of origami

- Turns paper into weaponry, dicing her enemies with paper swords and throwing stars

- Likes to sing to herself

As Paperstar enters the main lobby of the museum, Carmen's voice booms from the second-story balcony.

Museum's closed.

I'm here to give you your walking papers.

Oooh, papers.

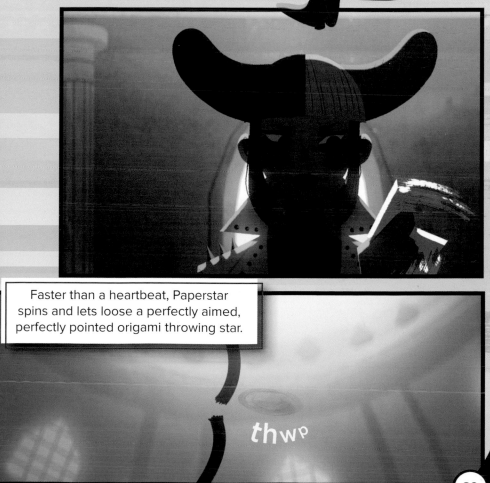

Faster than a heartbeat, Paperstar spins and lets loose a perfectly aimed, perfectly pointed origami throwing star.

thwp

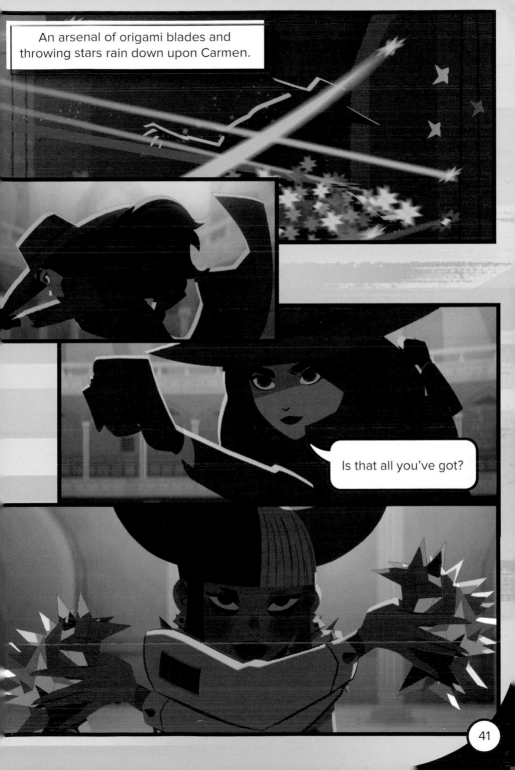

Paperstar unleashes a new volley of razor-sharp origami shapes. Carmen ducks, dives, and dodges her way through the barrage.

Finally, Carmen thinks she has found safety behind a column.

Ha!

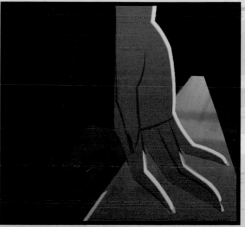

Paperstar reaches into her belt for more ammunition, but it's empty.

Out of ammo? That'll teach you to litter.

Paperstar pauses before noticing a stack of museum brochures on a nearby desk.

I really should reuse, reduce, and recycle.

Carmen dives for cover behind a statue as more projectiles hurl into its clay form.

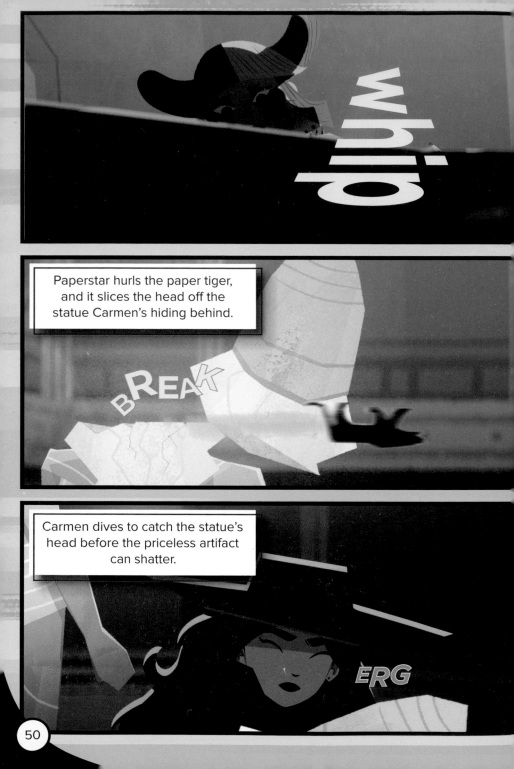

Paperstar hurls the paper tiger, and it slices the head off the statue Carmen's hiding behind.

Carmen dives to catch the statue's head before the priceless artifact can shatter.

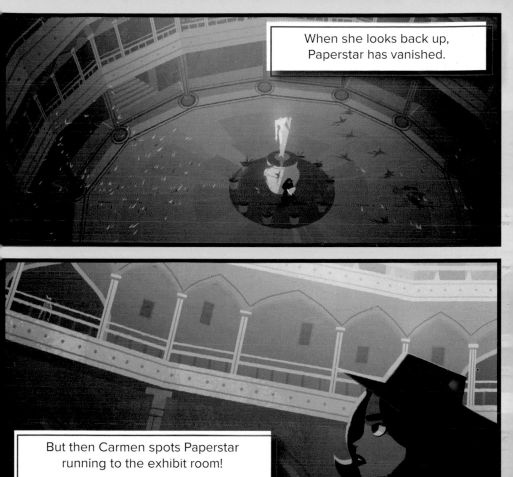

When she looks back up,
Paperstar has vanished.

But then Carmen spots Paperstar
running to the exhibit room!

Carmen carefully makes her way across the floor, scanning. There's no sign of Paperstar.

LA LA LA LA LA LA LA LA

From her hiding spot, Paperstar whips origami stars at Carmen.

whip

fWOOP

rustle
rustle

Carmen hears something and looks up, but it's too late!

Paperstar detaches a banner from the ceiling and rides it down, wrapping up Carmen in a giant "finger trap."

Such a pretty package...

...think I'll keep you under wraps.

Paperstar cuts a hole in the glass protecting the Magna Cartas.

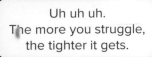

Uh uh uh.
The more you struggle,
the tighter it gets.

As Carmen watches Paperstar, she gropes for and finally finds the right tool to free herself.

Paperstar expertly rolls the collected delicate documents into a secure tube-shaped carrier with a strap that she slings over her shoulder.

Baaa bye, Little Black Sheep.

CLICK

Paperstar pulls the fire alarm and sirens blare.

Carmen finally manages to get loose and races after Paperstar.

Carmen emerges from the museum, and Paperstar is nowhere in sight.

Exhibit room at the museum, the next morning

It seems Carmen Sandiego has found some new hobbies...

Arts and crafts, and stealing historic documents!

It is origami -- the Japanese art of paper folding...

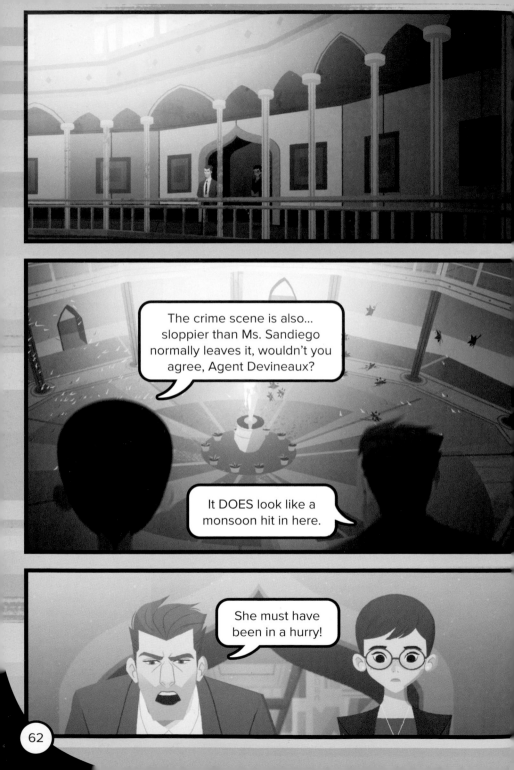

fWOOP

Chief projects in hologram form from Chase's pen.

Ahh! Greetings from Mumbai, Chief.

Agents -- I trust you were able to gain entry to the crime scene without incident?

This toy is incredible -- we were able to clear all local authorities away with one flash.

Your ACME keycard will provide you with Level One clearance anywhere in the world -- and gets you 10 percent off your purchase at any company store.

Where can I find these stores, and do they carry bulk quantities of razor blades, cheese, or breath freshener?

Ehh, ahem -- yes, the case.

ACME has just obtained this surveillance footage...

...taken from the café across the street. Unlike the museum, their security cameras weren't disabled.

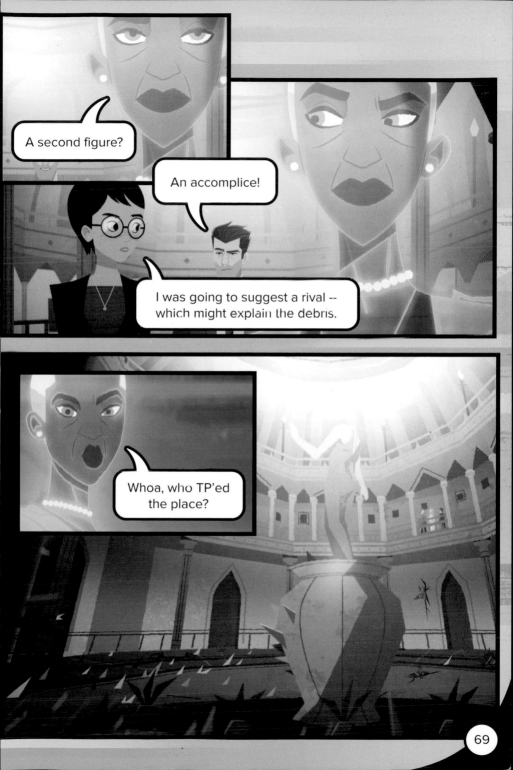

This way, no one operative knows too much about any given job. If they get nabbed, they can only divulge so much information.

Well, don't sweat yet, Red.

I'm scanning all local surveillance and pushing my new facial recognition software to the max.

If she's still in India, I'll pin her down.

Le Chèvre

- Real name: Jean-Paul

- Master of the high ground, leaping through the air with the grace of a mountain goat

- With his amazing climbing skill, he can scale the side of a building in seconds.

- If you can't find him -- try looking up.

LA LA LA LA LA LA LA LA LA LA
I see I am not the only one who admires Mumbai's historic Elephanta Caves.

Ahem...

The fish swims at midnight.

I repeat, the fish swims at --

No need to speak in code.

Tell me where to escort this -- a designated safehouse outside this country's borders, I assume?

What?! That is not how it works -- protocol dictates that you give me the package to deliver!

Protocol exists to protect VILE, should an operative get caught.

You look like an operative who would get caught.

I have completed more successful missions than you, Pippi Punkstockings!

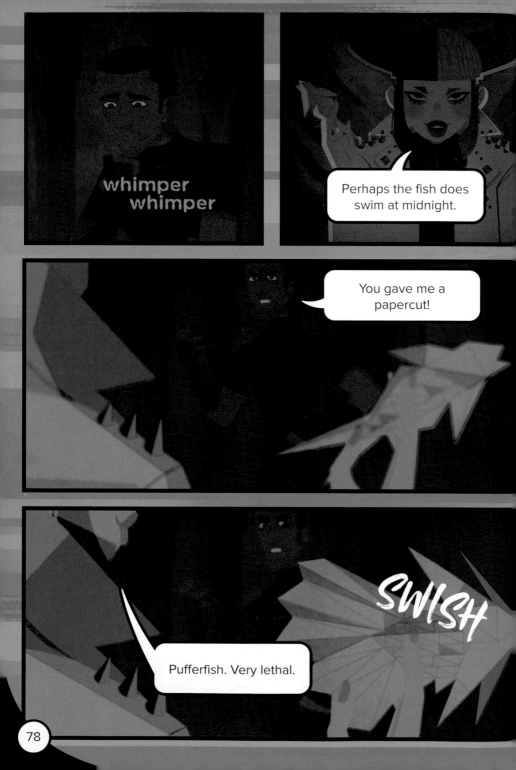

It will give you a thousand papercuts, unless you tell me the next drop location.
SWISH SWISH
Ouch!
No. Not my hands...

"Tammy Origami": she's going by an alias.

That's not too obvious.

It's Paperstar's way of saying, "come and get me if you dare" -- which suits me just fine.

Player, I need you to crosscheck that name against any mode of transportation you can think of: train tickets, plane tickets, car rentals --

Found her. "Tammy" bought a one-way ticket to Agra City on the 9:30 a.m. express train --

-- guess she wants to see the Taj Mahal.

Let's chase that paper.

Carmen walks down the aisle of the train, on the hunt for any sign of Paperstar.

Carmen enters a car undetected and slides into an empty seat where she can observe Paperstar from a safe distance.

Target spotted.

You gonna make a move?

In close quarters like this, with a wild card like her? Someone could get hurt.

I'll strike the moment she steps off the train...

Until then, I just need to stay out of her sight while keeping her in mine.

Carmen watches Paperstar like a hawk until her view is obscured by Chase, who suddenly plops down in front of her!

Ms. Sandiego, I presume?

Enough chitchat! Where are you hiding the Magna Cartas?

Me? Nowhere. But they are closer than you think.

Paperstar gets out of her seat and begins to walk to a different car.

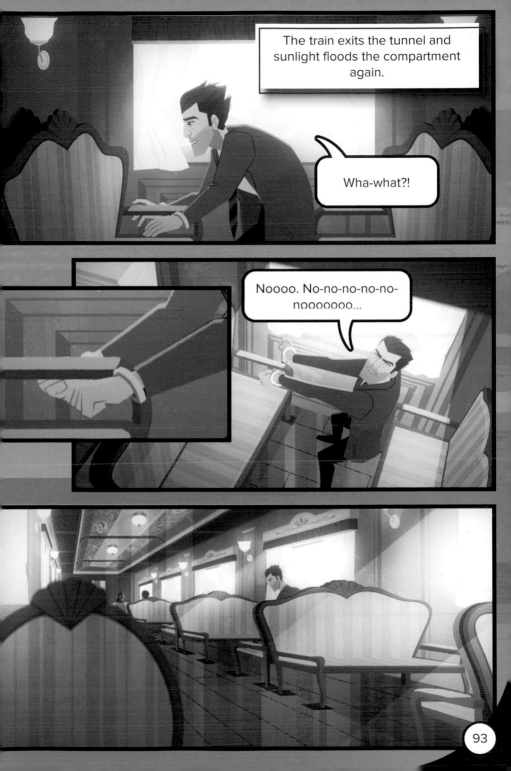

The door between cars slides shut, and Carmen pulls out Chase's ACME keycard, studying it.

"ACME," huh?

She pockets the card and continues to the next car.

Carmen pushes into the dining car and spies Paperstar sitting at the opposite end.

Improvising, Carmen darts into the first open seat she sees, her back to Paperstar.

This seat taken?

Actually, yes.

But, feel free to use it until my partner returns.

I see. And you are?

Julia.

So, Jules: off to see the Taj Mahal?

Carmen uses the reflection in a spoon to see Paperstar.

I wish -- the architecture, the history. Sadly, I'm traveling on business.

Carmen enters the first class section, walking down an aisle with enclosed private compartments to one side.

Paperstar freezes as she sees Carmen in the reflection of the glass.

She turns and hurls origami stars in Carmen's direction!

YAH!

Paperstar finally gets ahold of the magazine and tears it diagonally, ready to use it as if it were a blade.

Care to run now?

Good idea.

Carmen grabs
the Magna Cartas and runs
out the door.

Paperstar is not far behind.

Racing through train cars, Carmen reaches for another car's handle, but Paperstar is hot on her trail.

DING!

Carmen turns to climb to the roof.

119

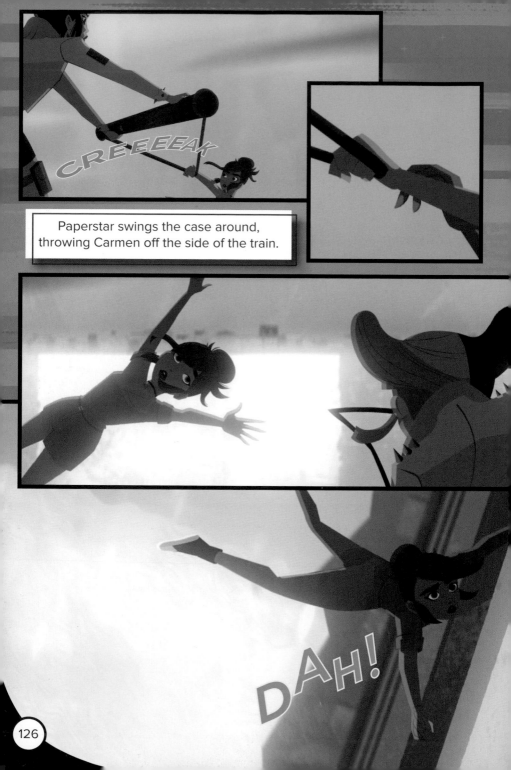

CREEEEAK

Paperstar swings the case around, throwing Carmen off the side of the train.

DAH!

Paperstar launches off the train with the tube and grabs onto the ladder with her free hand as the train continues to pass by below.

Carmen races toward Paperstar, determined not to let her get away with the Magna Cartas.

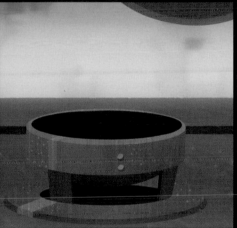

Here goes nothing.

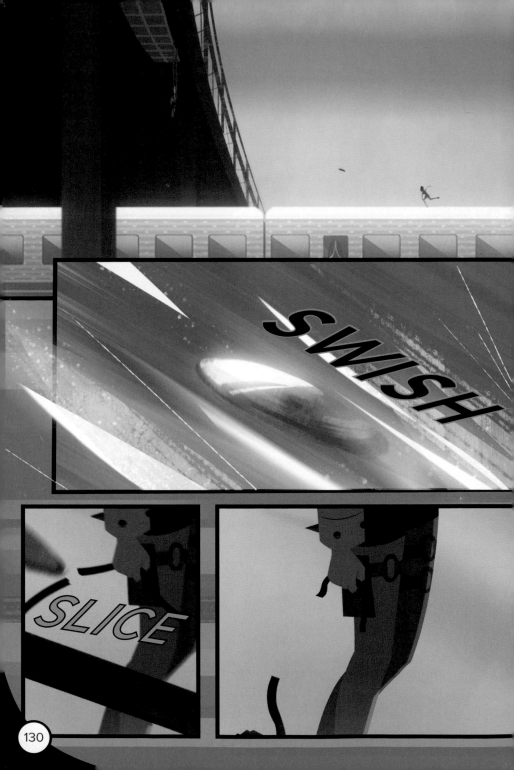

The train approaches Agra City.

Julia enters the dining car to retrieve Chase's briefcase, where she finds...

...the case containing the Magna Cartas!

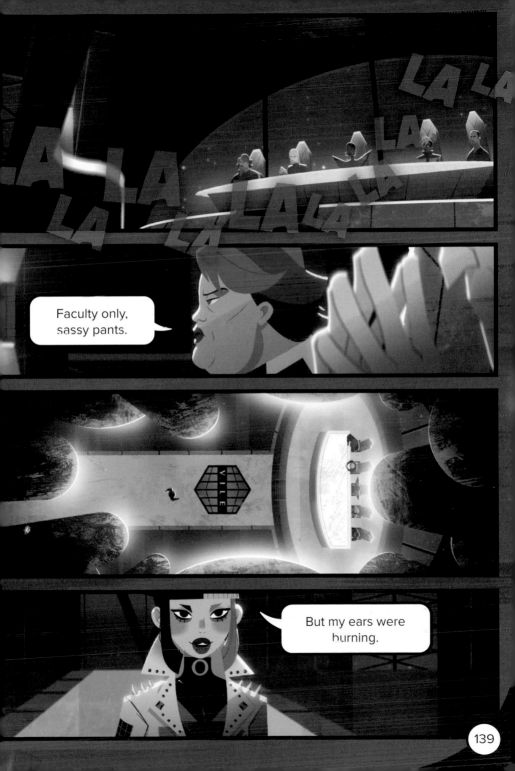

INDIA
DID YOU KNOW . . .

Capital: New Delhi

Population: 1.37 billion people

Official Language: Hindi

Currency: Rupee

Government: Federal parliamentary republic

Climate: India experiences a monsoon climate, characterized by strong winds that reverse direction, causing alternating wet and dry seasons.

History: The people of the Indus Valley built the world's first cities in what is now modern-day India. The region's history can be categorized by periods of Muslim, Hindu, and British rule before Mahatma Gandhi led a peaceful movement of resistance that resulted in the country's independence in 1947.

Flag:

Many people in India celebrate Diwali, or the festival of lights, as part of the Hindu New Year. They use clay lanterns to light their homes and pray for wealth and good luck.

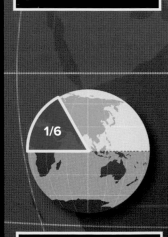

India is the second most populous country in the world, after China, and is home to one-sixth of the world's population.

Classical Indian music has three main parts, often played by instruments called the sitar, the tabla, and the tambura.

The Taj Mahal took more than 20,000 people and 20 years to complete and is designed with perfect symmetry so it looks the same from all sides!

Holi is a festival of colors celebrated across India to mark the beginning of spring and new life.

29,029 feet (8,848 meters)

The national animal of India is the Bengal tiger.

Roughly one-quarter of the country is forested, including regions of tropical evergreen forests, regions of tropical moist deciduous forests, and areas that are a mix of both.

The Himalayan mountains form the border between India and China and are the tallest mountain range on Earth. They include Mount Everest, which is 29,029 feet (8,848 meters) tall!

LOOK FOR MORE ADVENTURES WITH THE WORLD'S GREATEST THIEF!

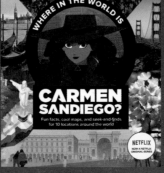